Snow Story

by Nancy Hundal
Illustrations by Kasia Charko

HarperCollins*Publishers*Ltd

HarperCollins Publishers Ltd,
Suite 2900, Hazelton Lanes, 55 Avenue Road
Toronto, Canada M5R 3L2.

For information address
http://www.harpercollins.com/canada
Printed in Hong Kong

97 98 99   First edition   10 9 8 7 6 5 4 3 2 1

Canadian Cataloguing in Publication Data

Hundal, Nancy, 1957–
Snow story

ISBN 0-00-224388-1 (bound)
ISBN 0-00-648095-0 (pbk)
I. Charko, Kasia, 1949–
II. Title.

PS8565.U5635S66 1997   jC813'.54   C97-930960-3
PZ7.H85Sn 1997

For my parents,

John and Doris Ferguson,

who gave me a childhood worth writing about.

Nancy Hundal

To Thomas and Kasia.

Kasia Charko

At first, the snow fluttered in like a secret. From her high window, Chloe watched snowflakes dance outside the glass. Then suddenly the snow hurtled down, poured from a cloudy pitcher above. No more secret.

Snow over hedges, over clotheslines and over toys left in the yard. Piled in little places you couldn't even see, and dumped in the middle of the lane where cars stumbled and tripped. It snowed out a birthday party, Chloe's dentist appointment, school.

Snow-joyed, Chloe piled on her snow suit, mitts, scarf, toque and boots and pounced on the snow in her yard. She made perfect round snowballs and threw them at the trees and the breeze. She pushed, pounded, packed the snow, making a snow family by the swing set.

The snow pushed back, made Chloe's toes so cold that she thought they'd snap off like icicles inside her boots. So in she went, took off her boots, toque, scarf, mitts and snow suit. Then Chloe rubbed her icicle toes.

From her window the next morning, Chloe saw a world that was white and still, a smooth piece of drawing paper. "Waiting for me!" Chloe sang. She rummaged in the kitchen—picked this, plucked that—then found her snow suit, mitts, scarf, toque and boots again. Chloe the artist was ready to emerge into the snow.

First she plopped backward onto her canvas, flapping her arms and legs, winging a feathery shape into the snow. Then, fingers pocket-fumbling, Chloe searched for the food colouring. Snow paints! She scattered, she scooped. Heart pounding, almost there. One step back, two mittens clap, and "Good morning!"

"Good night," Chloe whispered later as she watched the world and her angel fade into a chilly darkness. "I know you'll melt and fly away in the spring. But don't go yet, not yet."

The third morning, Chloe watched a man across the street shovel snow. He pitched snow from the sidewalks, chased it off the stairs and hedges, and scolded it from the top of his car. But the snow just laughed at him, landing on his clean walk as he turned away.

Chloe also saw her mom below, shovelling. She watched as her mom worked a little, then threw back her head to feel the laughing flakes on her face. Right then, Chloe decided that there were two kinds of grown-ups: the ones who liked snow and those who didn't. She figured that the ones who did, also ate bubble-gum ice cream and didn't mind getting rained on, and that was the kind she was going to be.

Chloe knocked on the window, Mom smiled, waved her down. Then snow suit, mitts, scarf, toque and boots. "Let's sled before bed!" said Chloe's mom. Chloe grabbed the sled, park ahead, Mom behind.

Chloe and her mom made long lines from top to bottom with their sled. They rode down, climbed back—fell off!—cheeks pinched by the cold, noses bitten red. Then, as it tried to become night, a white glow seeped from the snow into the sky above, making the evening seem as bright as day. Chloe rode the sled home, pulled by her mom through the cold, bright twilight.

At her window on the fourth day, a glint of sunny gold far out on the ocean tugged at Chloe's eye. The gold lay like a warm, sugary glaze poured over the sea.

"Warm there, cold here," Chloe said, looking down into her yard. "I wonder if angels get chilly too?"

Then out she went, and followed the delicate track of a sparrow and imagined its song. She found the harmony of a cat's prints twisting back and forth over the bird's. She followed the tune to its end, then followed her breath to its end at her door and went back indoors. No gold, too silvery cold today!

Inside, Chloe bored through all her new Christmas toys, past three library books and four cotton-glued snow drawings. Then came baking thick sugar cookies with her mom, cut in bird and cat shapes. The only song they made was a steady drumming as Chloe's teeth crunch-crunched through feathers and fur. She watched the heavy snow from the window, and ate too many cookies.

That day, Chloe played all of her old games, then pulled out her baby toys and tried to have fun with them. She tried on her mom's clothes, and asked for some arithmetic questions to work on. But the games were too old, the toys too young, the clothes too big and the questions too hard.

The next day, the snow lay stretched over the world like an octopus, gripping the land greedily. To shut out the cold, Chloe pulled down her blind and taped onto it a picture of a sunny day.

"I'm tired of this white world," thought Chloe. "But not of my angel. Sneak away, snow, but angel, don't go."

Bored, lonely, Chloe phoned her school friends, her swimming-lesson friends, her ballet friends. She sent away four cereal box tops for a bow-tailed kite. She fingered her mom's seed packages and tried to remember where the garden was under that slumbering octopus. Chloe went to bed early, bored, lonely.

She was awakened in the middle of the night by a sparkle of light. She went to the window and, for a moment, saw a sequined shine mounting the cloudy ladder to the sky. Then blackness, and a sleepy Chloe found her bed and her dreams again.

In the morning, Chloe remembered the strange light. She ran to the window and was amazed at what she saw. A world of grassy green! It stretched and wiggled, surprised to find its blanket so suddenly missing.

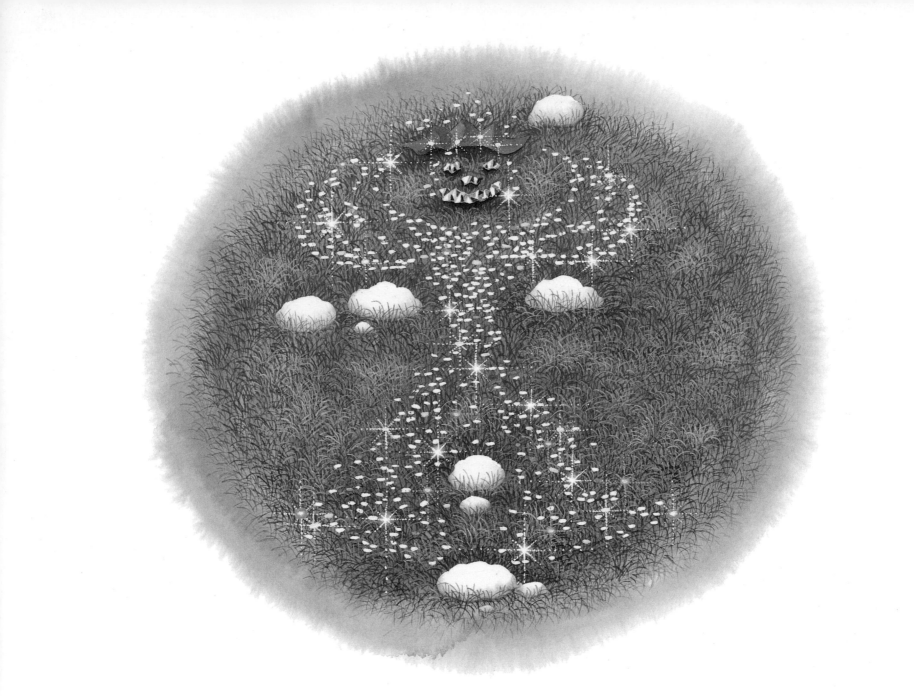

Chloe's angel had soared. The snow was gone.